Marissa
the Science
Fairy

To Sarah B, a true friend

Special thanks to
Rachel Elliot

ORCHARD BOOKS
338 Euston Road, London NW1 3BH
Orchard Books Australia
Level 17/207 Kent Street, Sydney, NSW 2000
A Paperback Original

First published in 2014 by Orchard Books

HiT entertainment

A CIP catalogue record for this book is available
from the British Library.

ISBN 978 1 40833 391 4

1 3 5 7 9 10 8 6 4 2

Printed and bound by CPI Group (UK) Ltd, Croydon, CR0 4YY

MIX
Paper from
responsible sources
FSC® C104740

FSC
www.fsc.org

The paper and board used in this paperback are natural recyclable
products made from wood grown in sustainable forests. The
manufacturing processes conform to the environmental regulations
of the country of origin.

Orchard Books is a division of Hachette Children's Books,
an Hachette UK company

www.hachette.co.uk

Marissa
the Science
Fairy

by Daisy Meadows

ORCHARD

www.rainbowmagic.co.uk

The Fairyland Palace

Fairyland School

Tippington Town

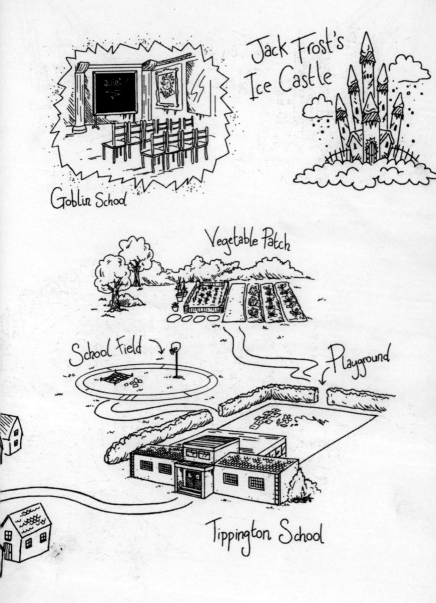

Goblin School

Jack Frost's Ice Castle

Vegetable Patch

School Field

Playground

Tippington School

Jack Frost's Spell

It's time the School Days Fairies see
How wonderful a school should be —
A place where goblins must be bossed,
And learn about the great Jack Frost.

Now every fairy badge of gold
Makes goblins do as they are told.
Let silly fairies whine and wail.
My cleverness will never fail!

Contents

Best Friends and School Friends!

Kirsty Tate smoothed down the jacket of her new school uniform and bit her lip.

"I feel excited one minute and nervous the next!" she said.

Her best friend, Rachel Walker, laughed and hugged her.

"Stop worrying," she said. "Just think how exciting it is that we are going to school together *for a whole week!* And you look really smart in my spare uniform."

It was the first day of the new term, and they were on their way to school. After weeks of late-summer storms and bad weather, Kirsty's school in Wetherbury had been flooded. It was going to take a week to get back to normal, and in the meantime her parents had agreed that she could stay with the Walkers. Best of all, she could go to Tippington School with Rachel!

"It's just a bit scary going to a new school," said Kirsty.

"But you'll be with me, in all the same lessons," Rachel reminded her. "Besides,

we always have fun when we're
together, don't we?"

Rachel always knew
how to cheer her
best friend up.

"I have the best
times with you,"
Kirsty replied
with a laugh.
"We've had lots of fun
adventures with the fairies, haven't we?
Oh, Rachel, wouldn't it be amazing if
our fairy friends visited us at school?"

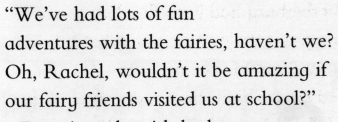

Ever since the girls had met on
Rainspell Island, they had kept the secret
of their friendship with the fairies. They
had often visited Fairyland together,
and the fairies had taken them on many
magical adventures in the human world.

"Look!" said Rachel, noticing three people waving at them from further down the street. It was her friends Adam, Amina and Ellie.

"Hi, Rachel!" they called. "Hi, Kirsty!"

Kirsty had met them on one of her visits, and when they smiled at her she instantly felt more comfortable.

"Have you moved to Tippington?" asked Amina in an excited voice. "Ooh, I hope so!"

"Not exactly," said Kirsty with a laugh. "My school got flooded, so I'm staying with Rachel until it's fixed."

"Well I hope it takes ages," said Ellie with a grin.

"Me too," said Rachel. Kirsty had a feeling that going to school with Rachel was going to be really good fun! The first day back at school was always exciting, but because the girls were together it felt like a holiday.

When they arrived at school, they sensed a real thrill in the air. Everyone was wearing carefully pressed uniforms and carrying brand-new bags. Shoes were shining and hair was neatly combed. The school secretary was trying to keep everyone organised, but she was in a bit of a flap.

"Ah, Rachel Walker!" she said, waving a clipboard in the air. "Is this your friend who is with us for a short time? Welcome, dear! Now, you are going to be in Mr Beaker's class this year, and your classroom is number 7. Hurry along, girls, and don't be late for registration!"

Adam, Amina and Ellie were also going to be in Mr Beaker's class. Together, they all went to find the classroom. They were lucky to find a table for five at the side of the room, and they all sat down together. Kirsty had just taken out her new pencil case when the door opened and a tall,

curly-haired man walked in carrying a
briefcase. Everyone stopped chattering
and sat up very straight. Kirsty and
Rachel linked their little fingers. What
sort of teacher was he? Would he be
fair? Would he be strict?

"Good morning, class," he said in a friendly voice. "I am Mr Beaker. Welcome to the start of a brand-new school year. I hope you're all looking forward to learning lots and having fun this term."

He smiled, and his brown eyes twinkled.

"He seems nice," whispered Rachel.

Kirsty nodded, but she didn't dare to whisper anything back. Mr Beaker opened the register and started to call out the names. He had just got to Kirsty's name when the door burst open and two boys leapfrogged into the classroom, giggling as they fell in a heap.

Mr Beaker's smile disappeared.

"Boys, you're late," he said. "Stop

messing around and find a seat."

Kirsty nudged Rachel.

"That's odd," she said in a low voice. "Have you noticed? They're in the wrong uniform."

The New Boys

The boys were wearing green blazers, and their green caps had extra-long peaks that hid their faces. They swaggered to a couple of spare seats at the back of the classroom.

Mr Beaker finished calling the register, but the two late boys weren't on it. He closed the register and looked at them thoughtfully.

"I suppose you're new to the school," he said. "You'll have to get the Tippington School uniform, and take off those caps. The pupils here don't wear hats."

"But our green uniforms look loads better than the stupid Tippington colours," the first boy complained.

"We've got notes to say we're allowed to wear our caps," shouted the second boy.

Rachel and Kirsty exchanged shocked glances. Neither of them had ever spoken to a teacher like that. Mr Beaker didn't look very pleased, but at that moment the bell rang.

"Time for assembly," said Mr Beaker. "Come on, everyone, let's go."

The class walked down the corridor in pairs, heading towards the school hall. Rachel and Kirsty were behind the two new boys, who were giggling and shoving each other. Everyone else was quiet, but the new boys didn't seem to care. The first boy elbowed his friend into the wall.

"Oops, sorry," he said with a cackling laugh.

His friend shoved him back, giggling.

"Whoops, didn't mean it!" he said in a singsong voice.

The first boy held out his foot and tripped up the second boy, who staggered sideways with a snort of laughter.

"Enjoy your trip?" asked the first boy.

Expecting the second boy to play the same trick, Kirsty looked down at their feet. In shock, she nudged Rachel, who gasped. The boys had enormous feet, just like goblins!

"They can't be!" Rachel whispered. "What would goblins be doing at Tippington School?"

In assembly, the children formed neat rows on the floor. Rachel and Kirsty sat next to the goblin boys, who were now playing tug-of-war with a pencil case.

"I still can't believe that goblins have joined our school," said Rachel in Kirsty's ear. "Maybe they are just ordinary boys with really big feet."

Before Kirsty could reply, Miss Patel, the head teacher, stood up. Everyone stopped talking, and Miss Patel smiled.

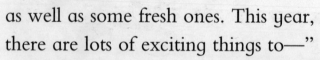

"Welcome back to a new school year," she said. "It's good to see lots of familiar faces, as well as some fresh ones. This year, there are lots of exciting things to—"

Miss Patel broke off and stared at the new boys. They weren't taking any notice of her.

"I want to hold it!" the first boy was saying.

"Give it to me," whined the second, pulling the pencil case towards him.

"Boys, put that pencil case down and be quiet," said Miss Patel in a sharp voice. "You may be new, but I'm sure this behaviour was not allowed in your old school. It's not a very good start."

The boys dropped the pencil case and folded their arms, looking sulky.

"Now, we need you *all* to be on your very best behaviour this week," Miss Patel continued.

"A school inspector is visiting here in three days to see how well we are doing. Your teachers will be giving gold stars to any particularly good work you do, and it will be displayed for the inspector. We want to show off your skills and talents, so let's all start the new year by trying really hard."

Kirsty and Rachel were so excited to hear about the gold stars that they stopped thinking about the big-footed boys. Then, straight after assembly, Mr Beaker took the whole class outside to the school vegetable plot.

"We're going to start with a science lesson on plants," he said as they walked across the playground. "I want you to find specimens to bring back to the classroom. Then we will look at them under magnifying glasses. I saw lots of vegetables when I checked the plot this morning, so you will have plenty to choose from."

"I love science," said Amina, catching up with Rachel and Kirsty. "I hope I can get a gold star for this."

"I wonder who will get the first gold star in our class," said Kirsty.

Just then Mr Beaker let out a surprised cry. The children at the front gasped.

"What's wrong?" asked Rachel, craning to see over the heads of her classmates.

Someone had trampled all over the school vegetable plot! It was a topsy-turvy mess of drooping plants and squashed vegetables. Some of the plants had been pulled up and then replanted upside down, so their roots were sticking

up in the air. Everyone stared in shock at the awful scene.

"I can't believe it," said Mr Beaker.

"Who could have done such a mean thing?" asked Adam.

Kirsty and Rachel had a very good idea who was responsible. At the back of the group, the new boys were stifling giggles with bony hands. Then one of them grabbed the pencil case from the other, and they started squabbling again.

"They are definitely goblins," said Kirsty, catching a glimpse of a long nose.

"But what are they doing at Tippington School?" asked Rachel. "And why have they spoiled our vegetable patch?"

A Trip to Fairyland

Mr Beaker wanted to carry on with the science lesson, so after they had tidied up the vegetable patch, they went back to the classroom. Rachel and Kirsty were given a dried-up bean to look at through their magnifying glass.

"Draw a picture of everything you can see through the magnifying glass," Mr Beaker told the class.

Kirsty and Rachel peered at the
shrivelled bean through the glass.

"That's odd," said Kirsty. "It should
look bigger through the magnifying
glass, but it looks smaller!"

"Same here,"
said Ellie, who
was trying
to draw a
squashed
radish.
"I can
hardly see
a thing."

"There's
something
wrong with the
magnifying glasses," said Adam, giving
his a shake.

"*They* don't seem to be having any trouble," said Amina, looking at the disguised goblins.

The first goblin was using his magnifying glass to look into the second goblin's ear.

"Yuck, it's all hairy and waxy!" he groaned, sticking out his tongue.

The other goblin grabbed the magnifying glass and peered up the first goblin's nose.

"Well this makes *your* nose look even bigger than usual," he said. "And it's full of bogies!"

"Keep the noise down, please," said Mr Beaker.

The goblins took no notice, and Kirsty frowned.

"Why is *their* magnifying glass the only one that's working properly?" she whispered.

"Amina, please could you water the plants on the windowsill?" asked Mr Beaker. "They're all drooping."

Amina filled the watering can and carried it towards the plants, but water started to drip from the bottom. It was leaking!

The carpet was soaked and so were Amina's shoes.

"Never mind," said Mr Beaker. "We've an extra pair of shoes here, and I'll find a spare watering can at lunchtime. Now, everyone take a ruler and measure one of the plants. We're going to keep a record of how much they grow this term, starting today."

Rachel and Kirsty thought that this sounded like good fun. They picked up their rulers and went to measure the plants.

"This can't be right," said Rachel. "My ruler says that this plant is two metres tall!"

"My ruler says that it's two millimetres tall," said Kirsty, examining the ruler. "Rachel, look! All the numbers are jumbled up!"

"Mine too," said Rachel. "I can't measure anything with this."

All the rulers that Mr Beaker had given out were the same. No one could measure the plants, and Mr Beaker had to give up and move on to the next part of the lesson. He looked really disappointed.

"Rachel and Kirsty, please could you fetch the plastic plant pots from the cupboard outside the classroom?" he asked.

Feeling very sorry for their new teacher, the girls hurried out of the classroom.

"Poor Mr Beaker," said Kirsty.

"Nothing seems to be going right for him today, does it?"

Rachel bent down to open the cupboard, and then tumbled backwards as a tiny fairy fluttered out. She was wearing a cute denim dress and a purple T-shirt with an orange neck bow. Her long auburn hair was swept up in a half-ponytail, and she had a pair of cool, dark-rimmed glasses.

"Hello, girls!"
she said. "I'm
Marissa the
Science Fairy,
and I've come
to ask for your
help. There's a
big problem at
the fairy school.
Will you come to
Fairyland with me?"

"Right now?" asked Rachel.

Marissa nodded eagerly, and the girls
grinned.

"We'd love to!" said Kirsty.

After a quick glance along the corridor
to check that no one was coming,
Marissa made a figure-of-eight shape
with her wand. Two golden rings of fairy

dust appeared in the air and
touched gently upon the girls' heads,
like tiny tiaras. Instantly, the school
corridor disappeared and they found
themselves standing in a rainbow-
coloured room. They had been
transformed into fairies, and they
unfurled their beautiful wings in delight.

"Welcome to the Fairyland School,"
said a familiar voice behind them.

The girls whirled around and saw
Carly the Schoolfriend Fairy smiling
at them.

"It's fantastic to see you again, Carly,"
said Kirsty, hurrying to give her a hug.

They hadn't seen Carly since their
adventures with Tilly the Teacher Fairy.
She was standing with a small group
of fairies who the girls had never met.

Marissa took Rachel's hand and led her towards the other fairies.

"These are the other School Days Fairies," she said. "Alison the Art Fairy, Lydia the Reading Fairy and Kathryn the PE Fairy. We've all noticed that things are going wrong."

"What sort of things?" asked Kirsty.

"Well, in my science class, all the plants have died," said Marissa.

"The paint colours have got mixed up in art class," said Alison. "Everything looks a horrible sludgy brown colour."

"The words have disappeared from all the books," said Lydia.

"And all the young fairies are flying backwards in PE class," said Kathryn. "We really need your help."

A Disobedient Class

"I bet Jack Frost is behind all this," said Rachel, folding her arms.

The School Days Fairies nodded.

"He stole our magical gold star badges," Marissa explained. "We use them to make sure that all lessons are interesting and go smoothly. Without them, lessons are a disaster!"

"Why has he taken them?" asked Kirsty.

"He's using them to help him set up his own school for goblins," said Carly. "I thought that he would have been put off after he stole Tilly's magical objects, but he's still determined to run his own school."

"The worst thing of all is that Queen Titania and King Oberon are supposed to be visiting the fairy school in the next few days," said Marissa. "We wanted everything to be perfect, but without our magical star badges it will all go wrong."

"Let us help!" said Rachel. "We'll do everything we can to find your badges in time."

"That's just what I was hoping you'd say," said Marissa with a grin. "There's no time to lose. Jack Frost has set up his school inside the Ice Castle, and my magic can get us in there. Will you come?"

"Of course!" exclaimed Kirsty. "Let's go!"

"Good luck!" called Carly and the other fairies.

Marissa waved her wand and there was a dazzling flash of golden fairy dust. When it cleared, Rachel and Kirsty were standing on a balcony overlooking a large hall. Marissa was beside them.

"We've been to the Ice Castle lots of times, but I've never seen this hall before," Rachel whispered.

The hall was very grand, with pillars of white marble and carvings of Jack Frost on the walls. There were swags of red plush velvet, and a portrait of Jack Frost hung at one end of the room.

The hall was filled with uncomfortable-looking wooden chairs, and on each chair sat a goblin.

"Look at their clothes," said Kirsty in a low voice.

The goblins were all wearing the same green uniform as the new boys at Tippington School. They were fidgeting, pinching each other and squabbling. None of them was paying any attention to Jack Frost.

The Ice Lord was standing at the front
of the class, wearing a black robe and
an old-fashioned professor's hat. He was
trying to present a slide show on the
whiteboard, but he had to shout above
the noise of the chattering goblins.

The first slide was a picture of Jack Frost wearing glasses. A caption said:

JACK FROST: FAMOUS SCIENTIST AND INVENTOR

"Jack Frost invented absolutely everything!" he bawled. "He is a genius. Write that down, idiots!"

Only one goblin, who was sitting in the very front row, starting scribbling on a piece of paper. The others just screwed up their papers and threw them at each other.

"Sit down and shut up!" Jack Frost yelled.

"Come on," said Marissa. "He has no control over this class!"

She flew over the edge of the balcony

and swooped down to hover in front of
Jack Frost. Rachel and Kirsty were close
behind her.

"What are you
pesky fairies doing
in my school
room?" Jack
Frost exclaimed.

"We're here
to take back
our magical
star badges,"
said Marissa in
a brave voice.
"They don't
belong to you."

The girls thought that
Jack Frost might try to catch them, but
he just sat down and folded his arms.

"Well, tough luck," he snapped. "I haven't got them any more. So you might as well just clear off."

"Is that really the truth?" asked Rachel.

Marissa looked around at the unruly goblins.

"I think it *is* the truth," she said. "If he had the star badges, the class would be happy and well behaved."

Just then, two of the goblins held a third one upside down and dipped his nose into an inkwell. Jack Frost bounded to his feet with a cry of rage.

"Stop that right now," he yelled, "or I'll expel you and send you to the human world, just like those other two mischief-makers. Then you'll be sorry!"

Kirsty and Rachel looked at each other, thinking exactly the same thing. He must be talking about the two goblins at Tippington School!

Quickly, Rachel whispered their idea to Marissa.

"Perhaps they have one of the magical star badges," she suggested. "After all, their magnifying glasses were working when no one else's were."

"There's only one way to find out," said Marissa, raising her wand. "I'm taking us all back to your school – right now!"

Fairies in School

As usually happened when the girls visited Fairyland, time had stood still in the human world. They found themselves back in the corridor outside their classroom. Marissa had returned them to human size again, and she tucked herself into the pocket of Kirsty's school skirt.

"Here are the plastic plant pots that Mr Beaker asked us to fetch," said Rachel, peering into the cupboard.

When the girls returned to the classroom, Mr Beaker was handing out some pods that he had picked from the garden that morning.

"Everyone take a plant pot and open a pod," he said. "I want you to take out the beans and plant them. There is soil on each table, and I have drawn the instructions on the board. Have fun!"

Rachel and Kirsty sat down at their table and opened their pods.

"Mine's empty," said Rachel, feeling disappointed.

"Mine too," said Kirsty.

Almost everyone in the class had an empty bean pod. The goblins were the only ones who had found beans inside.

"Ha, we're loads better at this than the rest of you," said the first goblin, sticking out his tongue.

Everyone watched as the goblins filled their plant pots with soil and then planted their beans.

"Very good," said Mr Beaker as the goblins patted down the soil. "Now, over the next few weeks we will see tiny shoots begin to grow, and..."

Mr Beaker stopped talking because something amazing was happening. Green stalks were already bursting out of the goblins' plant pots – poking through the soil, growing thicker and taller in front of their eyes.

"Impossible!" gasped Mr Beaker.

"Magic," said Kirsty, as the beanstalks reached the ceiling.

"It's like something out of Jack and the Beanstalk," Adam exclaimed.

"Whatever they are, they can't stay in here," said Mr Beaker. "Adam, go and ask the caretaker to fetch them and plant them in the vegetable plot."

As Adam hurried out of the room, Rachel leaned closer to Kirsty.

"This *must* mean that the goblins have Marissa's star badge," she said. "Only a science badge would make plants grow that fast!"

"We just have to find out where they're hiding it," said Kirsty. "Think, Rachel. Think really hard!"

Mr Beaker walked around the room, placing a drooping plant on each table.

"I would like each of you to draw a picture of the plant and label the main parts," he said.

The girls opened their pencil cases, and suddenly Rachel froze. Then she turned to Kirsty, her eyes wide and sparkling.

"I think I know where the goblins have hidden the star badge!" she said. "Remember how they were squabbling over the pencil case earlier? Each of them wanted to hold it. I think the star badge must be inside!"

"I'm sure you're right," said Kirsty. "Good thinking!"

Mr Beaker was helping Amina, and he didn't notice the girls slip out of their seats and walk over to the goblins. Their pencil case was lying on the table between them.

"Excuse me," said Rachel, "could we borrow some colouring pencils for our plant pictures?"

One of the goblins put his hand on the pencil case and pulled it closer to him.

"These are our pencils," he said in a rude voice. "Use your own."

He pulled out a green pencil, and Marissa managed to peek into the pencil case. Among the green pencils, she saw a flash of gold.

"My star badge!" she whispered to the girls. "It's in there!"

Kirsty pulled Rachel behind the giant beanstalk, which had now filled the back of the room. All the other children were busy drawing, so no one saw where they had gone.

"We have to get that star badge back," said Kirsty, sounding very determined.

"Marissa, will you turn us into fairies again? Perhaps one of us will be able to fly into the pencil case without the goblins seeing us."

With a wave of Marissa's wand, the girls were once again fluttering in the air beside her. The classroom looked very different now that they were so small, and their classmates seemed enormous!

Keeping out of sight, Marissa and the girls zoomed under tables and around chair legs until they reached the goblins. As quietly and slowly as they could, they peered over the table top. The pencil case was lying open, directly in front of Rachel.

A Daring Plan

Rachel looked around. Every head was bent low over the drawing paper – no one was looking at her. It was now or never. She took a deep breath and swooped towards the pencil case. But just at that moment, one of the goblins looked up and saw her.

"Fairy!" he hissed, slamming his hand down on the pencil case. "Time to get out of here!"

He zipped it shut and clambered across the table, trying to reach the door. The other goblin followed him, and the fairies ducked under the table. They zoomed around the legs of their classmates, trying to stay out of sight, and keep up with the goblins' scampering feet.

Suddenly they heard a deep voice shout, "STOP!"

It was Mr Beaker, and he sounded very cross. The goblins froze.

"How dare you climb onto the tables?" exclaimed Mr Beaker.

His voice was very loud now that the girls were so small. He started to tell the goblins off, and the fairies hovered under the table beside them.

"This is our last chance," Kirsty whispered. "Look."

She pointed up at the goblin who was holding the pencil case under the table.

Moving as quietly as they could, Rachel and Kirsty edged closer to the pencil case. They picked up the metal pull and started to ease it along the zip. Slowly, slowly, the pencil case began to open. The girls could only hope that the goblin wouldn't feel the movement until it was too late.

Marissa waited until the opening was big enough to fit through. Then she darted inside. Kirsty and Rachel held their breath and waited...and then the little fairy came zooming out with the star badge clutched in her hand. It had already shrunk back to fairy size.

"We've got it!" she said in an excited whisper. "Come on – back to the beanstalk!"

When they were safely behind the beanstalk again, a wave of Marissa's wand transformed Kirsty and Rachel back into humans.

"Thank you both for helping me today," she said, her badge back on her dress, and her eyes brimming with happy tears. "Now the young fairies will be able to enjoy their science lessons again."

"It was our pleasure," smiled Kirsty.

"Tell the other School Days Fairies that we're ready to help them too," said Rachel. "Goodbye, Marissa!"

The little fairy waved her hand and then disappeared in a puff of fairy dust. Kirsty peered out from behind the beanstalk.

"Mr Beaker's still telling the goblins off," she said. "We can slip back to our table now."

Mr Beaker sent the goblins back to their table and told them to carry on drawing. A few seconds later, when he looked around the room, Rachel and Kirsty were working on a plant picture together. It was as if they had never left their seats.

At the end of the lesson, Mr Beaker came to look at the girls' work. They had labelled the root, stem and leaves, as well as several other parts of the plant. Kirsty had added a colourful rainbow over the top.

"This is excellent, Rachel and Kirsty!" said Mr Beaker. "This deserves a gold star. I'm going to include it in the special display for the school inspector."

Amina and Ellie smiled at the girls to congratulate them, but the goblins were jealous.

"What about ours?" they demanded.
"Ours in the best!"

They held up their picture, but it just
looked like a green scribble.

"Well, at least you've tried your best,"
said Mr Beaker.

The first goblin shoved the second one
so hard that he nearly fell off his chair.

"Where's the magic badge?" the girls
heard him hiss. "You've lost it!"

"You lost it!" snapped the other.

While they were arguing, there was a knock on the classroom door and the caretaker walked in.

"Where are these giant plants?" he asked.

Mr Beaker turned to point at the beanstalks, and found that they had both shrunk to the size of a small pot plant. His mouth fell open.

"But…but…they were huge!" he exclaimed.

The caretaker looked doubtful, but then all the children started to speak at once.

"They were enormous!"

"They filled up half the room!"

"They were like trees!"

The caretaker laughed and shook his head.

"Well, there's only one explanation," he said. "They must have been *magic* beanstalks!"

He walked out, shaking his head, as Rachel and Kirsty shared a secret smile. The caretaker had no idea that he was absolutely right!

"I wonder if there will be more fairy magic waiting for us tomorrow," said Rachel, as they tidied up and packed away their pencil cases.

"I hope so," said Kirsty. "There are still three more star badges to find... and I'm really looking forward to meeting the other School Days Fairies very soon!"

Now it's time for Kirsty and Rachel to help...

Alison the Art Fairy

Read on for a sneak peek...

"Lunchtime already!" exclaimed Rachel Walker, closing her maths book. "I wonder what sandwiches Mum has packed today."

"I can't believe I'm really here," Kirsty Tate said with a smile, "at school with you!"

Rachel nodded happily. Being in the same class as her best friend really was a dream come true! Kirsty normally went to school in Wetherbury, but heavy rain over the holidays had flooded the classrooms. Now the school was closed for a week while builders repaired the damage and cleaned it up again.

Mrs Tate and Mrs Walker had been chatting on the phone when Rachel came up with the idea of inviting Kirsty to Tippington.

Read **Alison the Art Fairy** to find out what adventures are in store for Kirsty and Rachel!

RAINBOW magic

Join in the magic online by signing up to the Rainbow Magic fan club!

Sign up today at:
www.rainbowmagicbooks.co.uk

Meet the
School Days Fairies

Marissa
the Science
Fairy

Alison
the Art
Fairy

Lydia
the Reading
Fairy

Kathryn
the PE
Fairy

Kirsty and Rachel are going to school together! Can they get back the School Days Fairies' magical objects from Jack Frost, and keep lessons fun for everyone?

www.rainbowmagicbooks.co.uk

Competition!

The School Days Fairies have created a special competition just for you!

Collect all four books in the School Days Fairies series and answer the special questions in the back of each one.

Once you have all the answers, take the first letter from each one and arrange them to spell a secret word! When you have the answer, go online and enter!

What color is Saffron?

_ _ _ _ _ _

We will put all the correct entries into a draw and select a winner to receive a special Rainbow Magic Goody Bag featuring lots of treats for you and your fairy friends. You'll also feature in a new Rainbow Magic story!

Enter online now at www.rainbowmagicbooks.co.uk

Have you read them all?

The Rainbow Fairies
1. Ruby the Red Fairy ☐
2. Amber the Orange Fairy ☐
3. Saffron the Yellow Fairy ☐
4. Fern the Green Fairy ☐
5. Sky the Blue Fairy ☐
6. Izzy the Indigo Fairy ☐
7. Heather the Violet Fairy ☐

The Weather Fairies
8. Crystal the Snow Fairy ☐
9. Abigail the Breeze Fairy ☐
10. Pearl the Cloud Fairy ☐
11. Goldie the Sunshine Fairy ☐
12. Evie the Mist Fairy ☐
13. Storm the Lightning Fairy ☐
14. Hayley the Rain Fairy ☐

The Party Fairies
15. Cherry the Cake Fairy ☐
16. Melodie the Music Fairy ☐
17. Grace the Glitter Fairy ☐
18. Honey the Sweet Fairy ☐
19. Polly the Party Fun Fairy ☐
20. Phoebe the Fashion Fairy ☐
21. Jasmine the Present Fairy ☐

The Jewel Fairies
22. India the Moonstone Fairy ☐
23. Scarlett the Garnet Fairy ☐
24. Emily the Emerald Fairy ☐
25. Chloe the Topaz Fairy ☐
26. Amy the Amethyst Fairy ☐
27. Sophie the Sapphire Fairy ☐
28. Lucy the Diamond Fairy ☐

The Pet Keeper Fairies
29. Katie the Kitten Fairy ☐
30. Bella the Bunny Fairy ☐
31. Georgia the Guinea Pig Fairy ☐
32. Lauren the Puppy Fairy ☐
33. Harriet the Hamster Fairy ☐
34. Molly the Goldfish Fairy ☐
35. Penny the Pony Fairy ☐

The Fun Day Fairies
36. Megan the Monday Fairy ☐
37. Tallulah the Tuesday Fairy ☐
38. Willow the Wednesday Fairy ☐
39. Thea the Thursday Fairy ☐
40. Freya the Friday Fairy ☐
41. Sienna the Saturday Fairy ☐
42. Sarah the Sunday Fairy ☐

The Petal Fairies
43. Tia the Tulip Fairy ☐
44. Pippa the Poppy Fairy ☐
45. Louise the Lily Fairy ☐
46. Charlotte the Sunflower Fairy ☐
47. Olivia the Orchid Fairy ☐
48. Danielle the Daisy Fairy ☐
49. Ella the Rose Fairy ☐

The Dance Fairies
50. Bethany the Ballet Fairy ☐
51. Jade the Disco Fairy ☐
52. Rebecca the Rock'n'Roll Fairy ☐
53. Tasha the Tap Dance Fairy ☐
54. Jessica the Jazz Fairy ☐
55. Saskia the Salsa Fairy ☐
56. Imogen the Ice Dance Fairy ☐

The Sporty Fairies
57. Helena the Horseriding Fairy ☐
58. Francesca the Football Fairy ☐
59. Zoe the Skating Fairy ☐
60. Naomi the Netball Fairy ☐
61. Samantha the Swimming Fairy ☐
62. Alice the Tennis Fairy ☐
63. Gemma the Gymnastics Fairy ☐

The Music Fairies
64. Poppy the Piano Fairy ☐
65. Ellie the Guitar Fairy ☐
66. Fiona the Flute Fairy ☐
67. Danni the Drum Fairy ☐
68. Maya the Harp Fairy ☐
69. Victoria the Violin Fairy ☐
70. Sadie the Saxophone Fairy ☐

The Magical Animal Fairies

71. Ashley the Dragon Fairy ☐
72. Lara the Black Cat Fairy ☐
73. Erin the Firebird Fairy ☐
74. Rihanna the Seahorse Fairy ☐
75. Sophia the Snow Swan Fairy ☐
76. Leona the Unicorn Fairy ☐
77. Caitlin the Ice Bear Fairy ☐

The Green Fairies

78. Nicole the Beach Fairy ☐
79. Isabella the Air Fairy ☐
80. Edie the Garden Fairy ☐
81. Coral the Reef Fairy ☐
82. Lily the Rainforest Fairy ☐
83. Carrie the Snow Cap Fairy ☐
84. Milly the River Fairy ☐

The Ocean Fairies

85. Ally the Dolphin Fairy ☐
86. Amelie the Seal Fairy ☐
87. Pia the Penguin Fairy ☐
88. Tess the Sea Turtle Fairy ☐
89. Stephanie the Starfish Fairy ☐
90. Whitney the Whale Fairy ☐
91. Courtney the Clownfish Fairy ☐

The Twilight Fairies

92. Ava the Sunset Fairy ☐
93. Lexi the Firefly Fairy ☐
94. Zara the Starlight Fairy ☐
95. Morgan the Midnight Fairy ☐
96. Yasmin the Night Owl Fairy ☐
97. Maisie the Moonbeam Fairy ☐
98. Sabrina the Sweet Dreams Fairy ☐

The Showtime Fairies

99. Madison the Magic Show Fairy ☐
100. Leah the Theatre Fairy ☐
101. Alesha the Acrobat Fairy ☐
102. Darcey the Dance Diva Fairy ☐
103. Taylor the Talent Show Fairy ☐
104. Amelia the Singing Fairy ☐
105. Isla the Ice Star Fairy ☐

The Princess Fairies

106. Honor the Happy Days Fairy ☐
107. Demi the Dressing-Up Fairy ☐
108. Anya the Cuddly Creatures Fairy ☐
109. Elisa the Adventure Fairy ☐
110. Lizzie the Sweet Treats Fairy ☐
111. Maddie the Playtime Fairy ☐
112. Eva the Enchanted Ball Fairy ☐

The Pop Star Fairies

113. Jessie the Lyrics Fairy ☐
114. Adele the Singing Coach Fairy ☐
115. Vanessa the Dance Steps Fairy ☐
116. Miley the Stylist Fairy ☐
117. Frankie the Make-Up Fairy ☐
118. Rochelle the Star Spotter Fairy ☐
119. Una the Concert Fairy ☐

The Fashion Fairies

120. Miranda the Beauty Fairy ☐
121. Claudia the Accessories Fairy ☐
122. Tyra the Dress Designer Fairy ☐
123. Alexa the Fashion Reporter Fairy ☐
124. Matilda the Hair Stylist Fairy ☐
125. Brooke the Photographer Fairy ☐
126. Lola the Fashion Fairy ☐

The Sweet Fairies

127. Lottie the Lollipop Fairy ☐
128. Esme the Ice Cream Fairy ☐
129. Coco the Cupcake Fairy ☐
130. Clara the Chocolate Fairy ☐
131. Madeleine the Cookie Fairy ☐
132. Layla the Candyfloss Fairy ☐
133. Nina the Birthday Cake Fairy ☐

The Baby Animal Rescue Fairies

134. Mae the Panda Fairy ☐
135. Kitty the Tiger Fairy ☐
136. Mara the Meerkat Fairy ☐
137. Savannah the Zebra Fairy ☐
138. Kimberley the Koala Fairy ☐
139. Rosie the Honey Bear Fairy ☐
140. Anna the Arctic Fox Fairy ☐

The Magical Crafts Fairies

141. Kayla the Pottery Fairy ☐
142. Annabelle the Drawing Fairy ☐
143. Zadie the Sewing Fairy ☐
144. Josie the Jewellery-Making Fairy ☐
145. Violet the Painting Fairy ☐
146. Libby the Story-Writing Fairy ☐
147. Roxie the Baking Fairy ☐

The School Days Fairies

141. Marissa the Science Fairy ☐
142. Alison the Art Fairy ☐
143. Lydia the Reading Fairy ☐
144. Kathryn the PE Fairy ☐

Giselle the Christmas Ballet Fairy

Meet Giselle the Christmas Ballet Fairy! Can Rachel and Kirsty help get her magical items back from Jack Frost in time for the Fairyland Christmas Eve performance?

www.rainbowmagicbooks.co.uk